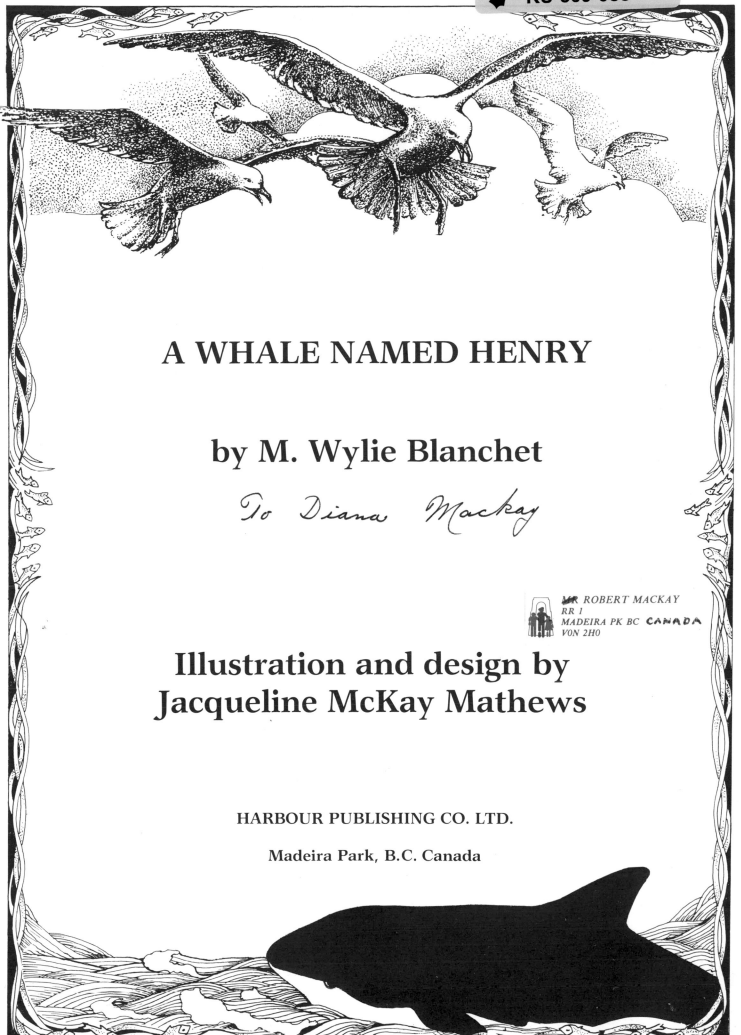

A WHALE NAMED HENRY

by M. Wylie Blanchet

To Diana Mackay

Illustration and design by Jacqueline McKay Mathews

HARBOUR PUBLISHING CO. LTD.

Madeira Park, B.C. Canada

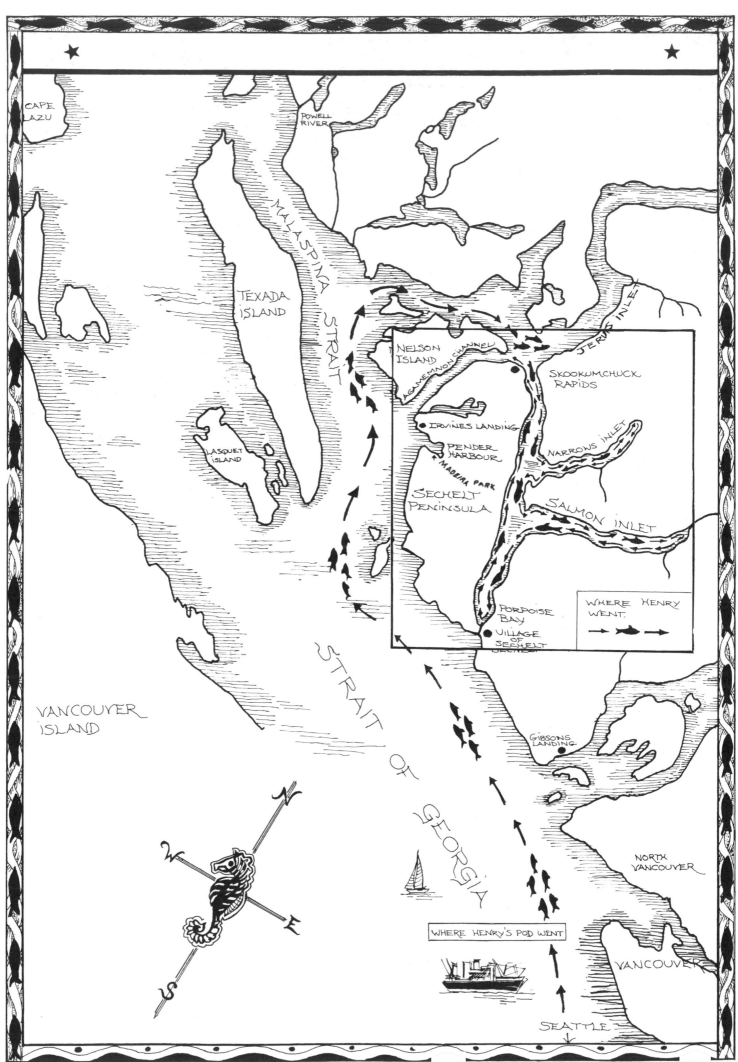

CAPE LAZU

POWELL RIVER

MALASPINA STRAIT

TEXADA ISLAND

LASQUET ISLAND

NELSON ISLAND

AGAMEMNON CHANNEL

JERUS INLET

SKOOKUMCHUCK RAPIDS

IRVINES LANDING

PENDER HARBOUR

MADEIRA PARK

NARROWS INLET

SECHELT PENINSULA

SALMON INLET

WHERE HENRY WENT.

PORPOISE BAY

VILLAGE OF SECHELT

VANCOUVER ISLAND

STRAIT OF GEORGIA

GIBSONS LANDING

NORTH VANCOUVER

WHERE HENRY'S POD WENT

VANCOUVER

SEATTLE

Chapter One

Henry's mother was very worried. You would not have known it to look at her, for she was a twenty-foot killer whale, and on the outside of her great, buttery, black-and-white hide she looked as untroubled as a very large inflatable toy drifting along in the placid waters of Puget Sound. But Henry's mother *was* worried and it was because Henry wasn't.

Henry didn't have the sense to be worried when he should be. That was the trouble with Henry. It had always been the trouble with Henry, but it had been less trouble when he was an eight-foot calf than it was now that Henry had become a boisterous thirty-foot youth.

"It's not that Henry isn't smart, exactly, " she would say as she tried to explain the trouble to other mothers in her family group, or pod, as whales prefer to call it.

"Of course not," the other mothers would agree, rolling slightly in the warm, clear water to keep one or the other of their small black eyes on their own lively boys and girls. "Your Henry is very clever."

"Henry can think just like all whales can," Henry's mother pondered on in her ponderous way. "The trouble with Henry is, he doesn't think at the right time."

"Yes," said another killer whale mother, giving a flip with her flipper to slide cooling sea water along her sleek black side, "Henry thinks *after* he gets into trouble instead of *before*."

"Yes," all the mother whales agreed. "That's the trouble with Henry."

The pod that Henry and his mother belonged to numbered twenty-two whales and was led by a giant bull whale named Skookum Cecil, who had once been trapped by some fishermen in a tight little bay named Pender Harbour. The cleverest of all the whales, Cecil had been able to learn the language of men well enough to persuade one friendly fellow, with black hair like sun-dried seaweed all over his head, to cut the nets and let him go back to his pod. But ever since that close call the word had been out among killer whales who travelled up and down the coastline between Puget Sound and Alaska to stay out of narrow, land-locked bays where fishermen might be waiting with their nets.

Killer whales, with their great shark-like dorsal fins, powerful jaws and sharp spiky teeth, are feared by even the much larger humpback, finback and grey whales, and had prowled these inside waters, fearing no other living creature, until the men began hunting them with their fine, invisible nets that were so difficult to see.

As the pod moved northward, Henry's mother kept watching and worrying and warning her bumptious boy about the dangers of the coast as they passed them one after another. She told him of the huge freighters on the shipping lane in Juan de Fuca Strait, bound for the cities of Seattle, Victoria and Vancouver, whose great thumping propeller-blades could slice a soft young whale in two. She pleaded with him to steer clear of the brown-stained waters drooling from the pulp mills of Bellingham and Everett, or later on, Harmac and Powell River, whose poisonous wastes could give him a whale-sized tummy-ache. She begged him not to go near

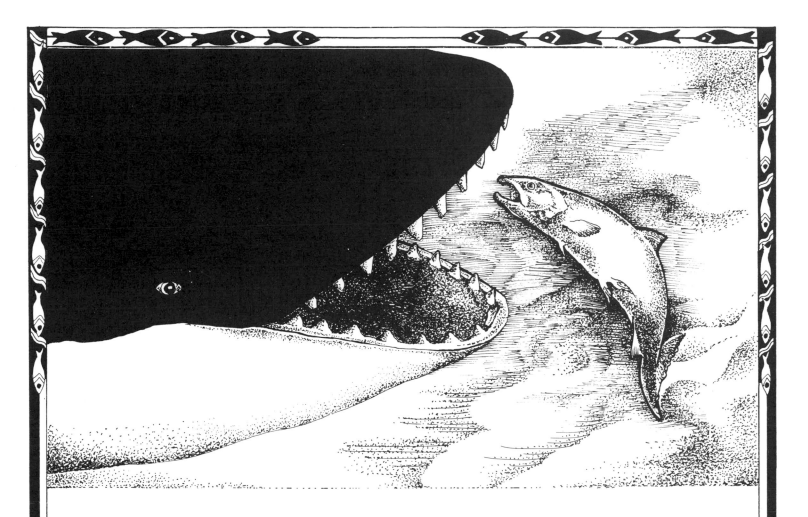

the shallow mudflats by the mouth of the great Fraser River, which could strand a reckless young whale before he knew it was happening, then as the tide went out leave him to bloat and die in the sun. But as the pod frolicked and splashed its way up the Gulf of Georgia, nervously darting past the mouth of Pender Harbour and gliding safely under the powerlines with their jolly orange balls high in the sky above Jervis Inlet, what worried Henry's mother most of all was that he would go chasing off after some fat frisky salmon and run right into one of these narrow-necked inlets or bays where the fishermen would corner him and take him away forever.

Henry's mother worried especially because the trickiest of all these narrow-necked inlets, the one people called Sechelt Inlet, was coming up right now on their right hand side.

"Henry!" she squealed in her highest pitched squeal, which is the way killer whales speak. "Henry!" She wanted to explain all the special dangers of Sechelt Inlet one more time: how it was a long steep-sided inlet that doubled back down the coast behind the Sechelt Peninsula and almost came out to Georgia Strait again at Porpoise Bay, but was blocked at the last moment by a low hump of sand. On the way down Sechelt Inlet on your left as you swam down toward Porpoise Bay, were two smaller inlets, the first one, Narrows Inlet, ending in a smelly mudflat and the second, Salmon Inlet, in a rushing waterfall. But the most confusing thing about Sechelt Inlet happened to you before you even got in it: the great, swirling, roaring tidal rapids at the entrance called Skookum Chuck. When the tide was coming in, the Skookum Chuck roared and swirled one way, dragging logs, boats, foolish young whales and everything else that came near, into Sechelt Inlet. Then when the tide started going out, the Skookum Chuck changed its mind and began roaring and swirling the other way, spitting everything back out of Sechelt Inlet into Jervis Inlet, where the pod was now. The Skookum Chuck could be very dangerous for an unwary young whale who had never known the wildness of a tidal rapids – he could be banged on the rocks, dizzied in the whirlpools and sucked in amongst all those mudflats and narrow places where he might never find his way out again.

"Henry!" his mother called, but Henry didn't pay any attention. To him it seemed his mother worried too much. After all, he was no longer an eight-foot baby. He was the largest whale in the whole pod, except for Skookum Cecil. It was time his mother realized he could look after himself, Henry thought.

Just then Henry's keen underwater hearing picked up the tinkling sound of a large school of salmon off to the right of the pod and he went streaking after them – heading straight towards the Skookum Chuck.

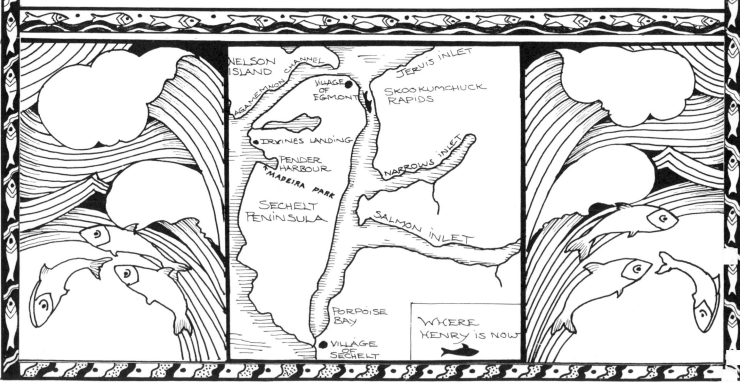

Chapter Two

"Puh-ph.. e.. w!" blew Henry in disgust. Another salmon had just escaped him, springing out of his way with a violent twist at the last moment. But frustration only served to make Henry more determined, and he plunged on after the school of great silvery fellows that raced and swerved through the deep waters of Jervis Inlet, always one leap ahead of him.

Then, "Puh-ph.. e.. e.. w!" blew Henry in alarm.

The salmon had vanished and Henry had turned to swim back the way he'd come, but he couldn't seem to make any headway at all. The current had suddenly become terribly strong and rough ripples pushed and pulled and jostled him. Just when he thought he had got the better of one, a bigger, rougher one would rush up and join the fight. Then, to his horror, he saw that the shore was going the wrong way! The village that had been almost beside him was slowly disappearing in the distance. Henry was being pushed backwards!

Frantically he redoubled his efforts but a whirlpool sprang at him with a wicked swirl and spun him round and round like a chip of wood, then sucked him down... round and round, faster and faster... down, down....

Then suddenly a straight current caught him, pulled him out of his whirl and threw him to the surface again. With a roar he expelled his breath, but before he could breathe in another monster whirlpool tore and sucked at him. He tried to hold himself limply like his mother had taught him, but the rest of his mother's lesson had been . . . *then dive deep and stay there!* But Henry couldn't do that here; in fact, he seemed to have no say in the matter at all.

"I'm getting mad!" sputtered Henry. "I won't stand for much more of this!"

"Oh, won't you?" roared the Skookum Chuck, filling Henry with water and tossing him sideways onto a jagged point of rock.

"Oh, won't you?" roared the Strong Waters, spinning him about and standing him on his head.

And they pulled and tore and fought and laughed as they tossed him along until, as his mother had feared, they threw him into that land-locked arm of the sea which is known as Sechelt Inlet; and there he lay, bruised and bleeding, a great battered hulk of a killer whale.

Henry lay motionless in a great bed of kelp, its cool, healing leaves pressing close about him. For three days he lay without stirring. But just when the crab and the rock cod, who were the chief inhabitants of that particular kelp bed, were working out how long it would take them to eat one whale, thirty feet by eight feet by six feet, if one seal, four feet by two feet, had lasted them ten days, Henry moved his tail. Not very far — just a fraction, in fact — but he could feel it all the way up to his head.

"O..O..O..!" he groaned.

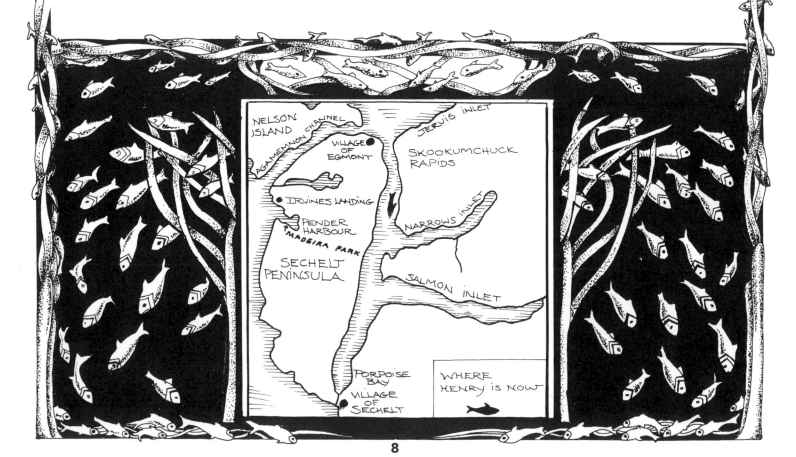

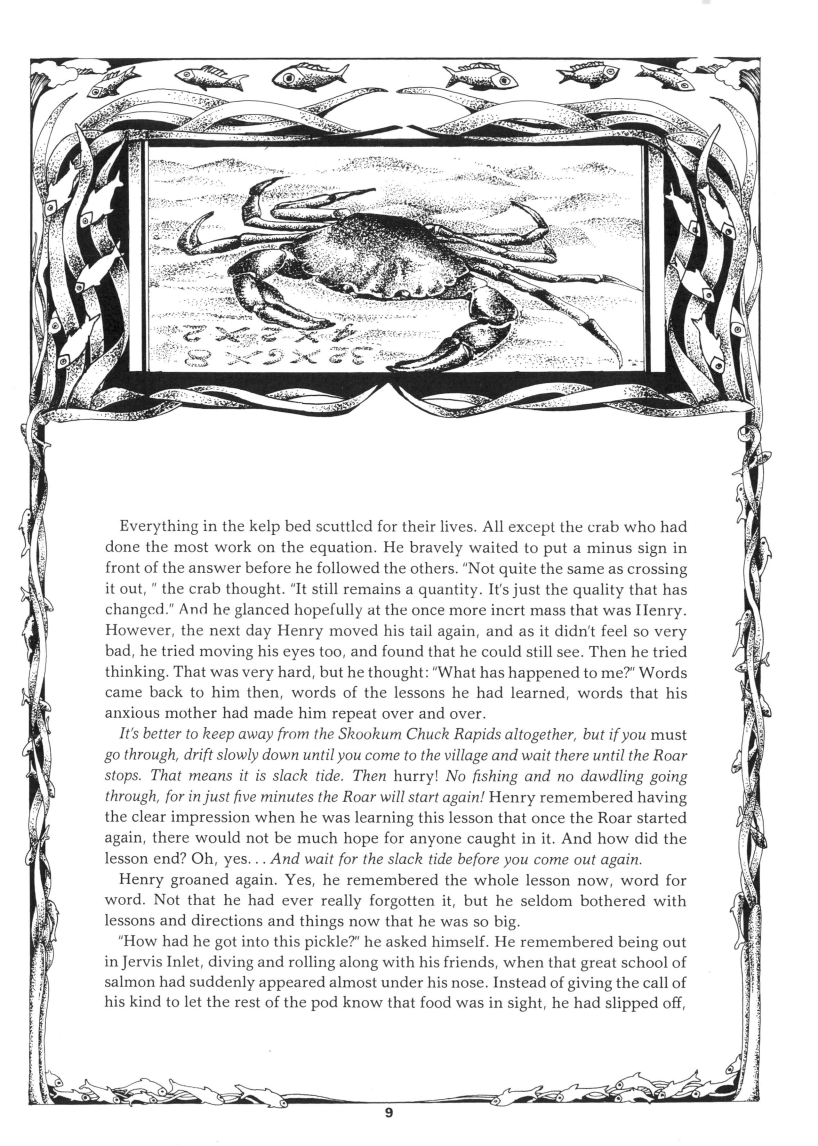

Everything in the kelp bed scuttled for their lives. All except the crab who had done the most work on the equation. He bravely waited to put a minus sign in front of the answer before he followed the others. "Not quite the same as crossing it out, " the crab thought. "It still remains a quantity. It's just the quality that has changed." And he glanced hopefully at the once more inert mass that was Henry. However, the next day Henry moved his tail again, and as it didn't feel so very bad, he tried moving his eyes too, and found that he could still see. Then he tried thinking. That was very hard, but he thought: "What has happened to me?" Words came back to him then, words of the lessons he had learned, words that his anxious mother had made him repeat over and over.

It's better to keep away from the Skookum Chuck Rapids altogether, but if you must *go through, drift slowly down until you come to the village and wait there until the Roar stops. That means it is slack tide. Then* hurry! *No fishing and no dawdling going through, for in just five minutes the Roar will start again!* Henry remembered having the clear impression when he was learning this lesson that once the Roar started again, there would not be much hope for anyone caught in it. And how did the lesson end? Oh, yes. . . *And wait for the slack tide before you come out again.*

Henry groaned again. Yes, he remembered the whole lesson now, word for word. Not that he had ever really forgotten it, but he seldom bothered with lessons and directions and things now that he was so big.

"How had he got into this pickle?" he asked himself. He remembered being out in Jervis Inlet, diving and rolling along with his friends, when that great school of salmon had suddenly appeared almost under his nose. Instead of giving the call of his kind to let the rest of the pod know that food was in sight, he had slipped off, intending to keep them all to himself. Then the salmon had swerved sharply to the right and he had followed, never quite catching up, always missing them by one leap. On they had raced... past the islands... leaping and twisting out of his way. He knew that they were heading straight toward the Skookum Chuck, the dangerous narrows through which the tide surged and roared in its efforts to fill and empty that great long arm of the sea, but he told himself that he'd have just one more try at them before he turned back. And this was the result.

He groaned and wallowed deeper in the soothing leaves. And the hopes of the inhabitants of the kelp bed ran high once more!

But the next day he felt decidedly better, and decidedly hungry. And in a couple of gulps, Henry swallowed all the inhabitants of the kelp bed with all their high hopes and their equation as well, although arithmetic really didn't interest him at all.

"That feels better!" sighed Henry. "Now I'll get out of here and go and find the others."

Away he cruised, but there was no sign of the place to get out and whichever way he turned, sooner or later he bumped into a cliff. So he stopped and repeated the instructions carefully, especially the last part: ... *and wait for the slack before you come out again.* Well, he was quite willing to wait for the slack all right, but first he had to find the place to wait for it.

"It's quite simple," said Henry firmly. "You wait for..." Bump! another cliff "... the slack and then you go out!"... Bump!

Chapter Three

When Henry was finished thinking, he had decided that instead of trying to find the Place to get out—which was difficult if you didn't know what it looked like—and then waiting for the Roar to stop, he would look for the Roar first. Once he had found the Roar, he'd have no difficulty finding the Place; for, of course, where the one was, the other would be too. Then he would get rid of the Roar by simply waiting until it stopped, and he would swim out through the Skookum Chuck and leave it behind. Henry felt very pleased with himself for having solved his problem so neatly.

"So now," he said, "all I have to do is swim along on the surface and listen. Once I hear the Roar, why I'm practically out!"

So hoisting his big black central fin well above the surface of the water until it looked like a spar buoy, and making as little noise as possible, Henry sailed calmly along in thirty-five fathoms of water just off the sheer edge of the cliffs.

Henry, of course, didn't know anything about the place he was in, except that as far as he knew there was only one way in or out of it. So he had decided that if he always kept the shore on his left side, he would always know that the next cliff was another cliff and not the same one. So every point he rounded, Henry would say, "And there's another cliff," and then he would listen very carefully.

However, after he had gone along for some time, the inlet got very narrow and he could see two cliffs, one on each side of him and very close together.

"And there's another cliff," said Henry very firmly. But he really didn't feel at all firm. Then he found that by closing his eyes and repeating to himself, "This is my left side," he could keep track of which was his cliff.

The current was a little stronger here, which made navigating difficult, especially since he was trying to keep one ear above water. Then suddenly he thought: "Current means Roar!" My goodness, what if this was the Skookum Chuck that he was in now, and suppose it suddenly began to Roar! Henry was so nervous that his whole tail trembled. Then to make matters worse, some seagulls began wheeling and calling to each other just above his head as though they anticipated a good meal. But Henry ignored them because he was becoming more and more certain that this was the Skookum Chuck, and he began racing ahead to get through before the Roaring began.

Henry's last doubts vanished when the inlet suddenly broadened out. "I'm out! I'm out!" he shouted to the gulls. "Thought I was going to make dinner for the lot of you, didn't you?" and he smacked his tail on the water and glared at them with his big white make-believe eye. Now he was off to find his brothers and he dived deep to make better time...

NELSON ISLAND
AGAMEMNON CHANNEL
JERVIS INLET
VILLAGE OF EGMONT
SKOOKUMCHUCK RAPIDS
IRVINES LANDING
PENDER HARBOUR
MADEIRA PARK
NARROWS INLET
SECHELT PENINSULA
SALMON INLET
PORPOISE BAY
WHERE HENRY IS NOW
VILLAGE OF SECHELT

Overhead the seagulls shrieked and laughed. "He'll go aground! He'll go aground!" "What a dinner we'll have!" "I bags first bite..." "No, I do! I do!"

Suddenly Henry shot up to the surface with a roar, hastily swallowed some water and blew it out with a frightful "Pu-ph-e-e-e-w!" which made the seagulls duck and whirl overhead.

"What's the matter with this water?" yelled Henry. "Rotten, funny taste!" And a moment later he roared, "And it's full of dirty, stinking, dead jellyfish!"

A couple of yards farther and he let out a terrific bellow and backed water with all his might. The water churned and became dark and muddy as Henry wallowed and blew, having realized at last that he had come up a blind inlet that ended in a fresh water river.

"Ha! Ha! Ha!" laughed the gulls, and one of them called out, "The tide's dropping! He'll get stuck!"

But Henry heard that exultant voice, and with a couple of snorts and another bellow, he started backing slowly out, hardly daring to breathe until he was back in deep water once more. There he rinsed his mouth again and again with the clean salt water, sending huge showers of it high into the air. He had never noticed how good it tasted before.

"Pu-ph-e-e-e!" he blew.

And off in the distance the seagulls called and shrieked, "Who cares! Who cares! Who cares!" but Henry didn't pay any attention to them at all.

Chapter Four

ather nice, this idling along by the light of the moon," thought Henry. Of course, Henry knew all about the moon. It had fallen out of the ocean down south and taken part of the sea with it. The hole that it left in the ocean was the same hole that the tides poured in and out of every day. Someone—he wasn't exactly sure who—had made a cover for the whole, and twice a day, that someone took the cover off the hole, and twice a day he put it back. Whenever the cover is open, the water rushes down and that makes the low tides and when the cover is closed, the water rises up again and makes the high tides. Yes, Henry knew all about the moon.

What's more, he even knew what he himself was made out of: yellow cedar. Well, maybe not Henry himself, but the first killer whale had been anyway, so Henry figured there was a good chance that he was too. Yellow cedar. Nothing else would do. Red cedar, hemlock, spruce—none of these could swim. Only yellow cedar. That's what the first killer whale had been made of 'way up north where the Indians named him Skana. All the other animals had been made by Raven, but Skana was different.

He had been made by an Indian named Natsayana, a long time after the other animals had been made. Natsayana had whittled him with a knife out of yellow cedar, and he had painted the big white eyes-that-weren't-eyes on each side of his head. Then Natsayana had told Skana to go and hunt for food—seal, halibut, salmon, anything that lived under water. But he was *not* to harm or eat human beings.

So Skana never did—at least, not since that first time when he accidentally upset two Indians in a dugout and ate them before he knew that they were men. Because he had eaten those men, he had become related to their tribe, and that tribe still uses the Killer Whale Crest for that reason.

Henry gave a prodigious yawn. No sleep for him tonight. Always this wretched listening for something that never came. But it was strange how many other noises he heard in the night. . . the p.p.p.pppppput of the little brown owls that flitted soundlessly except for the funny hu-hu-hu-hush of their wings. And the bats who could dart and dodge and miss anything by a fraction of an inch. Sometimes one of them would steal a mosquito that some other bat had intentions on and with high, terribly high squeaks, the rightful owner would dart after the thief. Down, down they would swoop, dodging around Henry's spar-fin until finally with one vicious little nip, punishment was meted out. Then, friends once more, they would chase off after the mosquito horde.

Several times Henry heard a shattering C--awk! and a great blue heron would rise slowly from the trees and flap off on its tremendous wings. It made Henry jump every time, before he remembered what it was. From time to time, he heard heavy smacks and plunges in the darkness around him. Someone else might have thought they were sounds made by enormous spring salmon; but to a trained ear like Henry's, the sound of fur striking water was quite different from scales striking water.

"Seals," Henry would say, his mouth watering. "Probably eating my fish, too!" And then he'd grumble, "They needn't be so noisy about it! Might as well be a barnacle the way I'm stuck on this cliff!"

Henry hated that cliff, but lose it he dared not.

The moon went down behind a mountain and after a while a cold grey light spread over everything. Seagulls began to drift above him, pale and wan against the silvery light, with sharp black edges to their wings. From the woods came faint twitterings and chirpings, and when Henry rounded a bend he came suddenly on a mink that was shrieking and scolding at a couple of young ones. It was still dark enough to see her eyes dartle red fire as she turned to glare at him. She didn't know what he was, but she was prepared to bite him anyway if he came any nearer.

"Pou. . ph!" said Henry, and all three of them fled for their lives under a rock. "Humph," said Henry, "I *am* rather big."

Lighter and lighter it grew until Henry could make out a deep bay just ahead of him, and he decided that it would make a good place to stop for breakfast, as he could hardly get lost in a bay. So, putting on an extra spurt of speed, Henry just dropped in.

Now it is rather an awkward thing for a small bay when a thirty-foot whale drops in for breakfast, but it is very much more awkward for the inhabitants of the bay, who in this case were mostly rock cod. Henry had a low opinion of rock cod because they lazed around in the shallow water and gossiped with the spider crabs in the kelp beds—"nasty, spiny things" he called them—but he was not in a position to be particular this morning. So-o-o, green cods, grey cods, brown cods, cods of all sizes and complexions, in they all went and the whole bay tossed and heaved with the commotion Henry made over his breakfast.

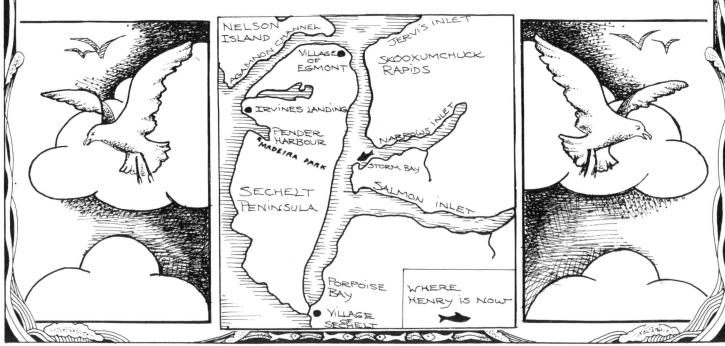

When at last he was finished, he vanished around the corner of the bay into the inlet again; after which the bay's remaining inhabitants got together and counted heads and dismally wondered if it were worthwhile beginning again.

Henry felt better with his belly full and he took a long deep dive to wash off the crawly feeling eating those wormy codfish gave him. He was already down at the bottom before he remembered his beastly cliff, and he made full speed to the surface again. He gave a sigh of relief. Still there, and just where it should be.

Off he went again. Same old side — same old cliff — same old Henry — same old everything. He had to find his Roar so he was very careful. In fact, he was so careful he travelled along almost scraping the cliffs.

Toward evening his carefulness was rewarded, for he *heard* something. At first, he didn't know what it was, but he knew it was a sound that hadn't been there before. He went very cautiously. The inlet was narrower now. Everything more or less as he had expected it would be. It was certainly beginning to sound very like you-know-what, all right. (He didn't dare say it, in case that made it stop.) Round another corner... still narrower... still louder. And then he was *sure*. This was the Roar!

"I'm out!" he shouted, trembling with excitement. "Well, practically out. Nothing to do now but wait for the Roar to stop!"

And easing himself in closer to the cliff, he settled down to wait for the tide to stop coming in or going out, whichever it was doing at the moment. That part didn't matter; what mattered was that it would soon stop doing anything and that would be slack water and the Skookum Chuck would stop roaring and foaming and he could swim safely out to rejoin the pod.

Henry shifted and sighed. He put one flipper up and the other down. Then he wriggled his big spar-fin to get the pins and needles out of it. How long should Roars take to stop? It seemed to him that he had been waiting a very long time. Still, with freedom so near, one must be patient.

He wished he could go a little nearer to the Roar, just to have a peek, but he didn't dare. Suppose it should catch hold of him and suck him down? He had got through alive once, but he didn't suppose that even a killer whale could do it twice. And even if he could, he certainly didn't want to. Once was enough for any whale.

He crowded in closer to the cliff. There was no ledge here and the rock went straight down for ten fathoms. He could see a vein of white quartz in the rock and he followed its white gleam down, down, down, out of sight.

It began to grow dark. The Skookum Chuck was not the kind of place that you would choose to go through in the dark. But it looked as though he might have to, for the Roar would certainly stop before morning. No Roar, Henry reminded himself, meant slack water, and there are usually four slacks a day, though sometimes only two. But in either case, it would be slack once during the night.

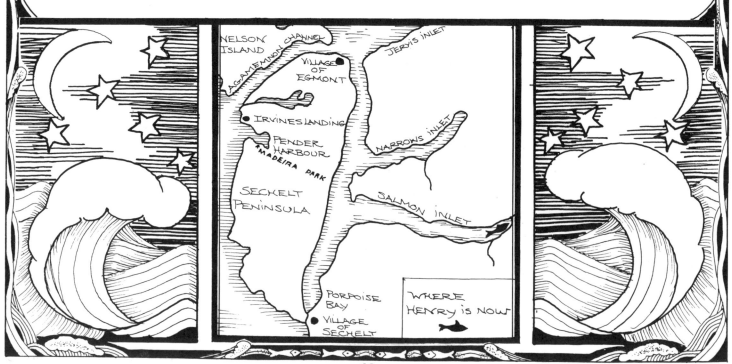

Chapter Five

It had been a long day and a tiresome one. Henry grew terribly sleepy. One by one, the stars came out, and as it got darker their reflections shone in the still deep water so clearly that sometimes Henry got quite bewildered trying to decide which were the real ones. The night was full of quiet little night noises, but Henry was so used to them by this time that they no longer surprised or interested him particularly.

He let out a terribly deep sigh and yawned... tremendously. This was the most monotonous thing he had ever done in his life. Stars, nothing but stars on all sides of him, all getting blurry and mixed up... joining together....

Splash! A cod flopped heavily somewhere behind him, and Henry jumped wide awake. He gave a snort of disgust when he realized he had been dreaming. Then his snort of disgust changed to one of dismay as he realized that if he had been dreaming, he must have been asleep. And if he had been asleep, he hadn't been listening to his Roar.

Now he listened hastily, but whatever had happened, there it was still roaring—a beautiful, steady Roar!

"Oh bother!" moaned Henry, "I must have missed my chance to get out!" And he vowed to listen more closely for the next time it stopped.

It was desperately hard to keep awake the rest of the night. The Roar, which should have helped, only made it harder, because its steadiness was like a drug on Henry. And it got worse every minute he listened to it. It had a way of coming closer and closer until it filled his ears, and gradually filled up all thirty feet of him. Then he began to swell up with it. . . bigger and bigger and bigger until he merged into the surrounding night, and felt himself floating away. . . .

Morning came at last. The sun rose up in a heavy mist, a sure sign of a hot day to come. Everything big and little had been up for hours about the affairs of the day. And what was more, everything was fed and comfortable. Everything except Henry. He still lay beside the cliff, pale and haggard, red of eye and tired of ear listening, ever listening, to his Roar.

At last he decided that, no matter what happened, he had to have something to eat. So, carefully working his way back half a mile to a place where he could still hear the Roar, he made a hasty breakfast of one unfortunate seal, three ling cod and two or three other odds and ends. Feeling very much better, he crept cautiously back to his place by the cliff.

He was absolutely convinced by now that the Roar must have stopped while he was asleep. There was no other possible explanation. But making some very rough calculations, he concluded that it was just about due to stop again—right NOW! So he got all ready for instant action—tail poised ready for its powerful strokes, and flippers prepared for the first dig. But after an hour of this, his tail grew tired and his flippers drooped, and Henry was forced to make some more calculations, basing them this time on a two-tide day. Then he relaxed; he had hours to wait.

Hotter and hotter grew the day. The smooth stone of the cliff beside him caught and held the heat. Or rather it held all it wanted and threw the rest away in a fiery blast that came to rest on Henry's great black back. His big fin began to droop like a candle that has been left in the sun. And the thick layers and rolls of fat that Henry was encased in became decidedly less solid.

Toward evening the cliff drew into the shade, and gradually Henry became aware of a rather peculiar thing. He should have noticed it hours before, but his brain had been as limp as his body. Now he could see that something was different. There were several well-defined marks on his cliff: the white vein of quartz, a green copper stain, and a crevice that held a plant of yellow rock-daisies. What Henry now became aware of was that they had not stayed in the same position. This morning early, he had been close enough to smell the daisies, and the copper stain had been right alongside him. He remembered touching a sudden bend in the quartz vein with his flipper. About noon, he remembered wondering if it were any cooler away up there where the daisies were, and from a distance, the copper stain had suggested cool, green ice. Now here was the copper stain right beside him again! And he could plainly see how the sun had parched and shriveled the poor little daisies!

"Oh no!" thought Henry. "I was up, then I was down, and now I am up again. That means the tide went out and now it is in again. But the tide can't go out and come in again without stopping for slack in the middle. . . but the Roar hasn't. . . or rather it has and it shouldn't have. . . or that is to say, it should. . . or rather it. . . ."

Here Henry put his head under the water to thicken up his brain again. Thoughts, he knew, shouldn't be quite as liquid as that! Fairly running all over the place, they were! Down in the cooler water, things gradually straightened themselves out, and his vague idea became a horribly solid thought: "something was wrong!"

There was nothing for it, he decided, as he came up to the surface again. He would have to risk everything and take a look at the Roar. Peering cautiously around each point before he rounded it, and never leaving one safe point until he was sure he could reach the next one, he started slowly toward the Roar. It got nearer and louder. Carefully he swung his tail out to try the force of the current. None! Goodness, his was a nerve-wracking job!

The next point jutted out very far. "Anything might happen once I get around it," thought Henry. He measured the distance with his eye and picked out a likely place for a back-current, then made a dash for it.

Safe!

Very warily, he peeked around the point, and straight across the inlet from him, he saw a deeply fissured cliff framed in a mass of evergreens. And from the fissure

poured a beautiful, roaring waterfall, churning the water below into a snowy whiteness.

"Such a beautiful roar," thought Henry bitterly," but it's not *my* Roar!"

The sun had sunk behind a mountain to the northwest, and the air was just pleasantly warm, as Henry raced away from the Falls. Slowly the hills were taking on that violet shade that would deepen to purple at a later hour. From the cool dark woods, the wood thrushes with their ringing, mounting notes called and called. A cicada droned and then stopped, remembering that the heat was past until tomorrow.

But all this was lost on Henry. He was red-hot and biting mad after a day and a half of waiting for a Roar to stop that didn't stop. A Roar that never had stopped and never would stop.

He was through for life with cliffs that led to nowhere. And he smacked the water with his mighty tail and dived down, down, ready to smash anything and everything that got in his way. Because somebody or something had made a fool of him, and somebody or something would have to pay!

Chapter Six

enry surfaced in front of a rocky point and paused to think, but just as he was about to get it all thought out a white goat trotted out onto a point of land and made the kind of noise that goats make. Henry stared. This was something entirely new to him. The creature made the noise again and came down onto the lower rocks and stared back at Henry. He didn't know what Henry was either, but whatever he was, he was company, and wherever he was going, the goat was going too. And he jumped and hopped and capered along the edge, with his sharp little hooves, going clack-clack-clack on the rocks. Whenever Henry stopped, he stopped too, and stood watching him, with his head and his ridiculous little beard tilted to one side.

Henry tried blowing at the strange creature, but it was just a waste of time, because the thing seemed to like it, and it hopped and jumped and capered even more.

The strait narrowed at this point, and out of his right eye, Henry could see a great high cliff looming over him. He glanced at his own left-eye cliff, but it was still very much the same: more pines, more arbutus, more rocks, all gentle and comparatively low. And then the strait opened out again.

"So peaceful," murmured Henry.

"Ye-e-e-e-es," agreed the goat, for he was anxious not to displease his new-found friend.

"Oh, shut up," said Henry rudely. "Can't you see you're not wanted?"

The goat cut a caper and stood on his head. The only thing that *he* could see was that he wanted company and Henry was better than nothing. He broke off a green shoot and nibbled it coyly.

"I'll race and leave the thing behind," Henry decided, and away he swam. The goat followed as best he could, but Henry soon left him behind, bawling piteously. Henry raced on through another retired strait, past another looming cliff.

"Ye gods! Another goat!" he cried. Well, he wouldn't give this one a chance to get familiar. He tore past at full speed, and the goat only had time to turn its head quickly from side to side to watch him pass. On and on he raced.

This was certainly a strange part of the inlet he was in. Every mile or so a narrow channel and huge frowning heights before the passage opened out again. And then another goat! The things were as thick as minnows in these parts. Henry put on an extra spurt and the goat never had a chance. He was making great old time now. . . .

Another goat! Henry blinked, but he didn't dare pause. But something was definitely wrong. He was beginning to feel all queer inside. Things were getting hazy in front of his eyes and he had a most peculiar light-headed feeling. He couldn't keep on at this pace much longer, goats or no goats. He had never felt like this before in all his life. . . .

It was narrow here, awfully narrow in fact, the narrowest yet. Could he make it? He made himself as skinny as he could to keep from scraping the cliffs, and staggered through.

Another goat! This was too much! He stopped with a lurch, and the whole world with the goat perched on top of it went round and round and round in huge circles. When the circles finally got smaller and at last stopped, everything swayed gently in front of him. Henry felt very sick.

The goat? Yes, the goat was still there, and Henry peered at it closely. It looked very much like the first goat that had paced him along the shore. But that had been miles and miles back.

From a dead branch above the goat's head, an angry kingfisher screamed, "Look here, you!"

"Who, me?" Henry asked.

"Yes, you," said the kingfisher, "What are you racing round and round our island for?"

Henry stared. "Island?"

"Yes, island! You've been round it a dozen times now, and you're upsetting everyone."

"Island," Henry said again slowly. "So that's why...."

The goat made his goat noise in a consoling sort of way, but Henry only glared at him.

"I must have mixed my sides up," he thought, but when he tried to untangle them, he couldn't. It was one of his off days.

Just then he remembered the dive he had taken after he had left the falls. That was it! That was how he had got going around the island!

"No more dives," said Henry with conviction.

"No more dives," agreed the goat.

"Oh, shut up!" said Henry and he swam off leaving the goat bawling mournfully.

The feeling began to sneak into Henry's mind that the cliff was not as friendly as it might be, and that it might trick him again if it got the chance. Well, there wasn't going to be another chance; Henry would take care of that. But there was no use staying where he was, now that he knew it was an island, so he crossed over to the mainland with its grim high cliffs that scowled down at their reflections in the water.

"Now," said Henry firmly, because he really wasn't really sure at all, "now, *this* is my left side." And off he swam.

The evening was cool and everything around was calm and peaceful, and beyond everything were the quiet purple hills and mountains. He found he liked it up here on top of the sea. He was so used to it now, with all his listening, that he rather missed it when he went down below. So he stayed up and settled down to a nice steady roll-a-long. . . roll-a-long. . . going nowhere in particular at all, when there, right in the middle of his path, was Timothy. And Timothy opened up his mouth and squawked at him.

"What?" said Henry, rather taken aback. Things, especially small things, didn't usually squawk at Henry.

"Squ-a-a-awk!" said Timothy again, and louder.

Henry was so astonished that he could only lie there and stare. And then, as he stared, Timothy opened his mouth again and held it open, quite plainly intimating that he expected Henry to give him something to eat.

This was absolutely too embarrassing. Henry, a killer whale, being asked to feed a bird! For it was a young grey seagull that floated on the water in front of Henry, looking at him with bright fearless eyes, and asking for something to eat. Henry glanced from side to side to see if anybody was watching.

"Squa-a-a-awk!" said Timothy once more and held his mouth open.

Henry wriggled his tail. "Look here," he protested, "don't you realize what I am? What's the matter with you anyway? Why aren't you flying?"

"I can't," answered Timothy. "See? I have a broken wing. A man mended it for me but it's still no good."

Henry looked. One soft grey wing had been broken just above the second joint. It had been carefully spliced with three matches, their heads still on, and bound with a piece of green fishing twine. Quite a workmanlike job, and evidently partially successful for the little gull could now hold that part of the wing against his body. The chief trouble now seemed to be the tip. Perhaps a tendon had been severed, for the tip of the wing with all the strong feathers needed for flying hung down limp and useless, trailing in the water.

"Humph!" said Henry, quite interested, and hoping that if he kept on talking the thing would forget about eating. "A man fixed it, you say?"

"Yes," nodded the seagull. "He found me on the beach, and carried me home and fed me. I stayed with him for a week. He was a nice man and he named me Timothy."

"Timothy?" echoed Henry. "Why did he call you that?"

"Because my toes are pink," answered Timothy.

"Oh?" said Henry. He wasn't used to such young pink things, and he eyed the gull nervously. Just then Timothy opened his mouth wide, once more asking for something to eat, and what was worse, evidently expecting to have it fed to him.

"I-I say!" protested Henry desperately. "I haven't got anything to eat and I wouldn't know how to feed you if I had!"

"Couldn't you catch me even one little fish?" pleaded Timothy. "I could eat it by myself if you caught it." And he squawked again.

That is where Henry made his first mistake. For he said, all right, he would get him one if he would keep quiet after that. Then he dived and presently reappeared with a nice grilse in his mouth. He put it in front of Timothy and hastily backed away.

But he needn't have worried. Timothy was quite equal to eating it himself, and tore it viciously to pieces—clutching, grabbing and bolting all he could hold. When he had finished, and had rinsed his beak and ruffled up his feathers as best he could with his broken wing, he turned confidently to Henry and said,

"Well, what shall we do now?"

Then Henry made his second mistake. He should have left at once, but instead he stammered, "Wha-at?" and he was lost. He tried to mend matters when the seagull repeated the question, by saying that he couldn't, as he had to find the way out, because he had forgotten to remember that he wasn't looking for it anymore.

"What way out?" asked the seagull.

"The way out of this inlet," said Henry gloomily. "You wouldn't understand," he added and turned away.

"Oh yes I would!" said Timothy brightly. "I've often been out of here!"

Henry turned and stared at him.

"Often been out," repeated the little seagull, nodding his head. "Often, often."

"And you'll show me?" asked Henry eagerly. "Show *me* the way out?"

And Timothy said, "Yes. But tomorrow, not tonight. I'm sleepy." And without even bothering to say goodnight, Timothy tucked his head under his good wing and went to sleep.

Henry was left there looking at a ball of grey feathers, and wondering if it were safe to trust a seagull who was called Timothy because his feet were pink. But as there was nothing he could do about it anyway, he decided that he would have a sleep too.

So, side by side out in the widest part of the inlet, they slept: Timothy, full once more and happy in spite of his broken wing, and Henry, worn out with listening and disappointments.

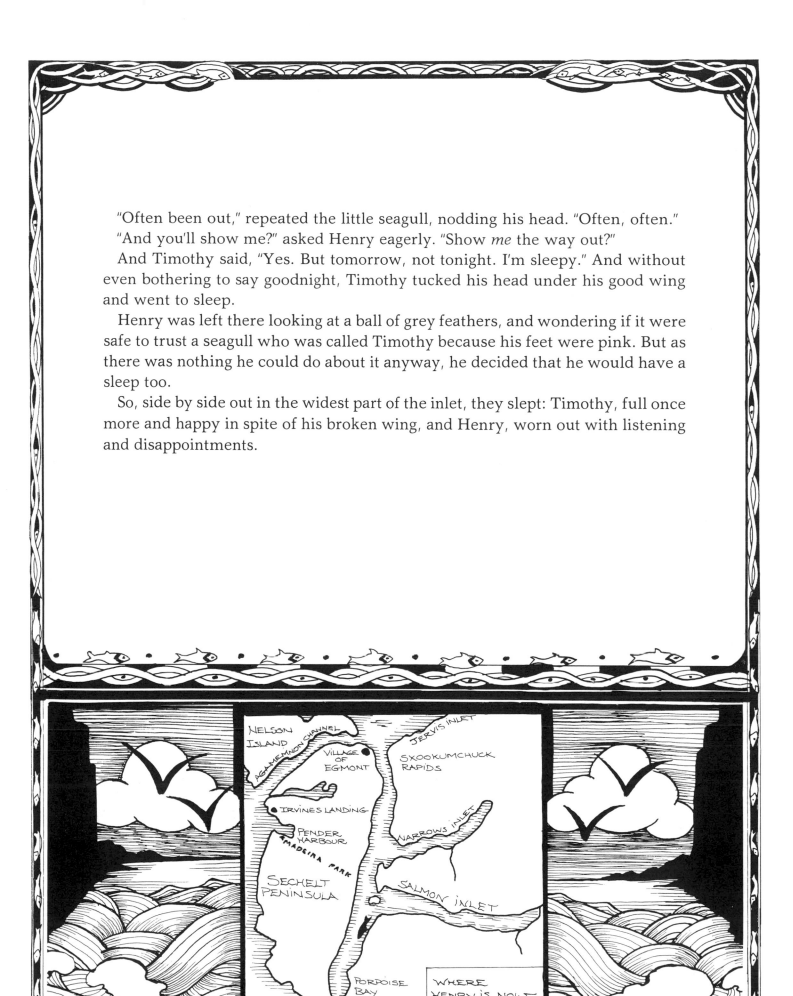

Chapter Seven

It was quite light—cold, grey, silvery light—when Henry woke up next morning—or rather was wakened up—and looked about him trying to figure out what had roused him.

"Squ-a-a-awk!" said a voice beside his ear, and then he remembered. Timothy, of course.

"I wish you wouldn't do that before I'm awake," grumbled Henry.

Most very small things would have felt rather alarmed to be grumbled at by a whale, but Timothy had no such sense. He merely ruffled up all his feathers, and looked so soft and downy that Henry felt like a bull, and *that* was a new feeling for Henry! Then Timothy opened his mouth wide, very wide, and kept it open. Henry knew what he was expected to do, but still feeling grumpy, he started to ask the gull what he thought he was. Thinking better of it, he told him instead to stay where he was and not move, and he'd go and find him something. Then he dived out of sight.

It took some time to find Timothy's breakfast as he thought he might as well eat his own while he was finding it, and it takes an awful lot of breakfast to fill up a killer whale. So it was always: "Oh, this will do for Timothy. No, no, it's too big!" Scrunch, gulp, smack! And so on, for quite a long time. However, finally he saw quite a small grilse.

"Just the thing for Timothy," he said, and as he couldn't possibly hold any more himself, he took the grilse very carefully in his saw-edged teeth.

The grilse didn't understand what was happening, since he had never been eaten by a whale before. Of course, he had thought about it—all fish do—but he had always supposed that it would be quite a sudden kind of death. And here he was still wriggling and able to think about it. How could he be expected to know that the whale had caught him for a seagull's breakfast, and that death was merely postponed? However, even a grilse believes that where there's life there's hope, so he held himself like a coiled spring, ready for his chance of life should it come.

"Now to find Timothy," said Henry through his teeth—he couldn't speak properly on account of the grilse, so his words sounded more like "Ow, oo fine Eo-o-hee."

He was beginning to worry that he might have come rather a long way in his search for breakfast, and he felt a little anxious as he rolled upward. He broke through the surface with a terrible snort, just as the sun broke through low clouds over a distant hill. He looked around in all directions, but there was no sign of one small gull waiting with its mouth open.

"Eo-o-hee!" he called as best he could. "Ee-o-hee! 'ere are 'ou?" Confound this grilse in his teeth.

"Ee-o-hee!" he wailed. "Kwi'! I 'ot 'or 'reakfas'!"

But still there was no answering squawk.

He tried blowing, hoping that might attract the seagull's attention, but the grilse interfered with that too, and he couldn't even give a decent blow.

"I just have to give one proper yell," he thought. "This fish is probably dead by now anyway."

"Timothy!" he shouted, and the cliffs echoed "Tim-othee-ee-ee-ee!" And then again from far off, "Timothee-ee-ee . . . Timothee-eee. . . . "

But before Henry had finished his shout, the grilse had made his spring for life. And before the last echo had died away, it was safely hidden at the bottom of the sea.

"Now he's gone and made me lose his breakfast," wailed Henry, after he had carefully searched all around, under his flippers and behind his tail. "Perhaps I've swallowed the thing," he thought hopefully, and he gulped a couple of times to see if he could feel anything halfway up or halfway down. But there was no answering lump. He saw a crowd of seagulls in the distance shrieking and yelling over a school of brit, and he swam toward them.

"Go away! Go away!" they screamed as he got nearer. And when he still came on, they all flew up in the air, which meant that Timothy couldn't be one of them. How they shrieked and threatened him for ruining their breakfast!

"Have you seen Timothy?" he yelled at them.

"Tim . . . othy Pinktoes! Tim . . . othy P . . . P . . . inktoes! Ha, ha, ha, ha, ha,

31

ha . . . " laughed the gulls.

This was more than Henry could stand. He turned tail and fled, followed by a shrill chorus of "P . . . inktoes! P . . . inktoes! P . . . inktoes."

He dived deep to shut out the sound and didn't venture to the surface again until he was a good mile away. Even then he listened to make quite sure that he was out of earshot.

"Ti-i-i-imothy!" he shouted, and again the cliffs caught it and tossed it from crag to crag up the mountainsides. "Ti-i-imothy! Ti-i-imothy" he screamed. "You've *got* to show me the way out!"

" . . . way out!" said the cliffs.

" . . . way out!" said the mountain.

" . . . way ou-u-u-ut," whispered the last crag and tossed it into space. But there was no answer from Timothy.

What was he going to do? How could one small seagull with a broken wing get lost like this just when he was needed most?

A tugboat worked its way along the shore to the south, rounding up a tow. "Timo-thy-timo-thy-timo-thy. . ." said its diesel engine, running slack with no load.

Henry pricked up his ears. "Did you say you had seen Timothy?" he asked as he came up alongside the tug. A man came out of the engine room and looked down at him.

"Timo-thy, Timo-thy?" repeated Henry impatiently.

"Hey, Pat!" the man called to someone in the engine room. "Come on up! Here's a friend to see you!"

A shock of red hair followed by a big square face appeared in the doorway. "Friend of *mine*?" he asked, eyeing Henry without enthusiasm.

"Well, just listen to him! He's making a noise that sounds exactly like that engine of yours!"

"Timo-thy, Timo-thy?" asked Henry anxiously. "Timo-thy?"

"He sure wants *somebody*," said Pat. "Hope he don't think it's me!" Then he yelled at Henry, "He ain't here! Ain't here, you savvy? Over there!"and he pointed to a tug in the next bay.

"Heaven help 'im if he finds 'im," said Pat as Henry started off.

Then Henry stopped. "Very strange!" he said, turning around and eyeing them again. There it was again. "Timo-thy-Timo-thy-Timo-thy. . ." blew the engine.

"I believe they've had him there all the time," he growled and he swam back and tried to look into the boat. But Pat saw him coming and turned on full compression.

The engine changed its note. "Stung-stung-stung-stung. . ." it boomed as the tug forged ahead. Henry decided he must have been mistaken, and he dived hastily out of the way.

He didn't ask the other tug. What was the use, when it probably didn't know its own mind either? Saying one thing one minute and another thing the next? No, he would just think. So he thought and thought, and then he thought and thought

some more. And by and by, he managed to think where he had been when he last saw Timothy—the same place they had gone to sleep the night before.

He looked around. There in the distance was the high cape to the south, with the low island to its north. Why, he must be within half a mile of the place!"

"Didn't I tell you I couldn't think?" he asked the inlet and the sky and the mountains, and off he went down the path of the sun at a terrific rate.

"Ti-i-i-mothy!" he shouted.

"Squa-a-a-awk!" said a voice right beside him.

Henry wheeled around. There was Timothy, still sitting with his mouth open, waiting for this breakfast, and looking very pathetic. Henry's joy at seeing him turned to consternation.

"B-b-ut," he stammered, "you made me lose your breakfast while I was looking for you."

Timothy didn't answer, merely opened his mouth wider and waited.

"Oh dear," worried Henry, "I suppose I'll have to get him something. But what if I lose him again? I'll try going straight down and straight up again."

Down. . .down. . .down. . . he went straight below Timothy. Twenty fathoms, thirty fathoms, and at forty fathoms he found just the thing—a bright red snapper who had felt quite safe at that depth. But what are forty fathoms to whales? Even two or three hundred are nothing to *them*. And so, although the snapper protested, Henry dragged him up to the surface and gave him to Timothy. And the little seagull got to work on the snapper without even saying thank-you.

When he had finished gorging himself, he rinsed off his beak and said, "Well, come along and I'll show you the way out now."

Chapter Eight

So on down the sun's path they went, Henry trying to keep from slipping along too quickly, and Timothy paddling and paddling and paddling with his little pink toes. But they had hardly gone more than half a mile before they were both exhausted, Henry from going so slowly and Timothy from going so quickly.

"You'll have to give me a ride," gasped Timothy, stopping to hold his sides.

"Me?" said Henry. "Me give you a ride? I've never given anything a ride in my life, and I'm not going to begin now!"

"You'll have to," panted Timothy, "or I can't show you the way out."

"Well, how do you want to travel," asked Henry sulkily, "in my mouth?"

"Of course not," said Timothy, "on your back. I'll climb on."

"Oh, all right," grunted Henry.

Then pat-pat-pat-pat-pat... cold pink toes pattered up his back, accompanied by much squawking and fluttering of the one good wing because Henry was *very* slippery.

"All right," said Timothy at last. "But go slowly. There's nothing to hold on to up here."

Henry gave a cautious roll forward, and Timothy slid sqawking along his back toward his head. Just as he reached Henry's blow-hole, Henry let out his breath and Timothy shot high into the air on a water-spout.

"Y-you beast!" he spluttered, as he flopped down into the water with a splash.

"Sorry!" said Henry cheerfully. "But it wasn't my fault."

"Of course it was!" snapped Timothy angrily. "Who ever heard of anyone having a waterfall in the top of his head, anyhow?"

"Perhaps you'd better swim, after all," offered Henry hopefully. But his hopes were soon dashed. Timothy promptly refused to stir another inch. For all he cared, Henry could stay in the inlet for the rest of his life.

"But I can't help it if I'm slippery," said Henry, "And if you're so stupid that you can't stay on, you'll *have* to swim."

"I *won't!*" said Timothy.

"Well, don't!" said Henry. "I'll find my own way out!" and he blew savagely.

And Timothy? Well, Timothy just ruffled up his feathers and put his head underneath his good wing. Henry's heart missed a beat. The last time Timothy had done that, it had meant a whole night's sleep before he had stirred. Still, Henry was darned if this miserable bird was going to boss him around.

"All right, goodbye!" he called cheerfully, watching Timothy carefully.

Not the slightest sign from Timothy to show whether he had heard or not. Henry backed slowly away. . . farther, and then farther. When he was about fifty yards away, he sang out, "Well, so long!" And he raised himself in the water to watch the effect. But there was not a sign from the round grey ball rising up and down so gently on the little waves.

"Darn him!" said Henry.

He decided to try frightening him to make him squawk for mercy. He raced toward the little grey ball, then tore round and round it, making huge tide-rips whose waves lept in all directions at once. But up and down, up and down, crest and trough, bobbed Timothy. Head over heels he turned at times, little pink toes looking so limp and helpless that Henry hated himself. Then he hated himself for hating himself. Miserably soft this inlet was making him! No way for a he-whale to feel at all!

But at last he could stand it no longer, "All right!" he shouted. "You can ride!"

From beneath his wing came Timothy's soft grey head with its bright little eyes. "I think I'll try riding behind your big fin this time," he announced calmly.

"Not even seasick," thought Henry in disgust. "All right, climb on," he growled.

"Oh, of course, if you don't want me. . . " began Timothy, glancing down at his wing again.

Henry groaned. "Of course I want you! I'd *love* to have you!"

"Well," said Timothy, brightening up immediately, "if you *really* want me. . . " and once more he started to climb on board.

Henry lay there, trying not to squirm, as pad-pad-pad went the little pink toes.

When the gull was settled behind the big spar-fin, Henry started off very gently with his usual roll. This was splendid! As he rolled, Timothy just leaned gracefully against the fin and all was well. But the next part of the roll took the wrong curve, and, squawking and fluttering, Timothy slid slowly back till he came to rest on the flat surface of the tail. He had hardly got himself steady there when s-s-s-s. . . he slid forward again toward the fin.

"Henry! Henry!" he shrieked as he collided with the fin. . . "Henry!" he screamed as he landed once more back at the tail, balancing first on one foot and then the other, his one good wing more trouble than help.

"Henry!" he screamed as he neared the fin once more.

"What's the trouble now?" asked Henry, looking around innocently. "You're riding, aren't you?"

"No!" sobbed Timothy. "I'm only gliding! You'll have to swim differently, or keep straight, or *something*!"

"I can try," said Henry doubtfully. "How's this?"

"Much better," sniffled Timothy, drying his tears.

So, in a cross between a shimmy and a wriggle, using his flippers instead of his tail, Henry crawled along at about one knot an hour. How thankful he was that none of his friends were here to see him! He, Henry Whale, reduced to such depths by this inlet that he was letting a seagull ride pink-toed over him, forcing him to slither along in this ridiculous fashion. Then he remembered how awfully soft and small Timothy was, and how his toes had looked so limp and helpless when he was turning somersaults. . . he brought his thoughts up sharply with a snort.

The very idea of a thirty-foot whale having thoughts like that! "Pink toes", he thought, "are only a means to an end!" And hopefully, that end would be Henry's escape from the inlet. But at this crawl, he very much doubted that they would ever get anywhere. Oh, for the wild, free life of the open sea again!

"Aren't we almost at the place to get out?" asked Henry.

"Do you see that point, the far one?" and Timothy pointed with his good wing.

Yes, Henry saw it quite clearly, and he calculated that with Timothy on his back, it was going to take three hours to reach it, whereas by himself he could do it in about three minutes.

"Well, around that point is Porpoise Bay, and *that* is where the way out is," explained Timothy.

Henry pricked up his ears. Porpoises made good, substantial eating. "Are there any porpoises there?" he asked eagerly.

"I don't know," answered Timothy impatiently. "I've never seen any. Now, hurry up."

Somewhat dampened in spirits, Henry started his miserable crawl-and-wriggle toward the distant point. Timothy enjoyed the ride. Henry did not.

But when they rounded the point, Henry stopped and not another wriggle would he make. There along the shore sat a row of cottages and in the water, people rowed about in boats. Go in there with a seagull on his back? Never. In vain, Timothy argued and pleaded and sulked. Finally, Henry agreed to go after it got dark.

"Dusk," said Timothy.

"No, dark," insisted Henry.

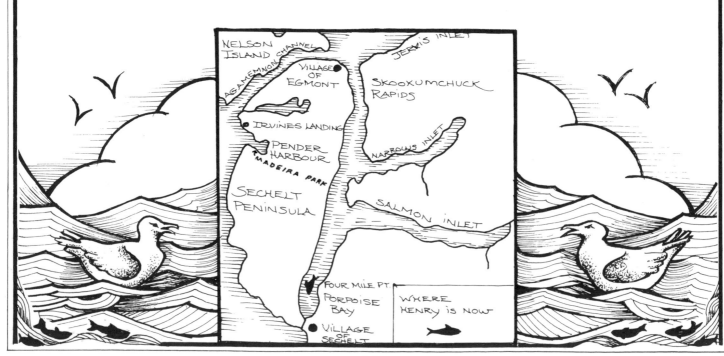

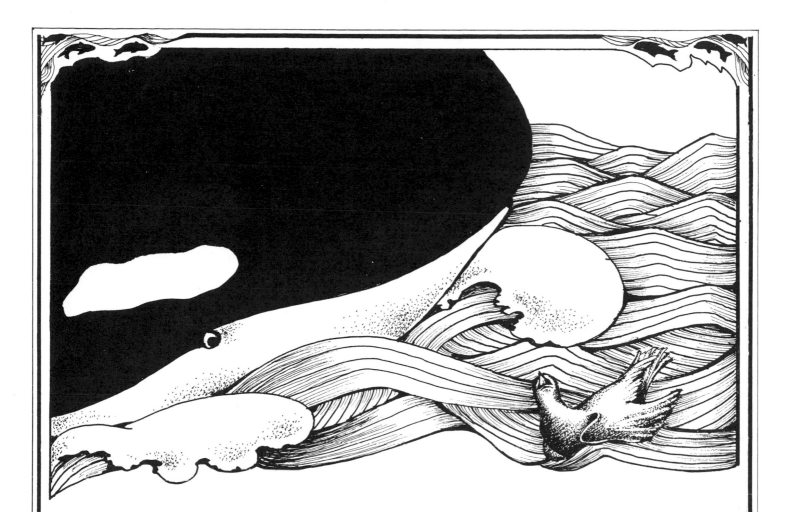

"Dusk!" repeated Timothy.

"Well, between dusk and dark," conceded Henry and looked so ugly that Timothy let it go at that.

In the meantime, while they were waiting for it to get between dusk and dark, Henry said that if Timothy would stay right where he was, that he would go and find himself something to eat.

"Squa-a-a-awk. . . " began Timothy—

"And you too, of course," said Henry hastily.

So Timothy agreed, if it wouldn't take too long.

The thought of porpoises was still lingering in Henry's mind, and he decided that he might as well look around the bay while he was at it. But it was just as well not to let Timothy know what he was up to, so he took a long dive that brought him up well around the point and out of Timothy's sight. There, Henry surfaced and blew with satisfaction, but there were such shrieks from all sides, and so many little boats making for the shore, that he soon gave up his idea of seeing the bay.

When he returned, there was Timothy up on the shore, terrifying the life out of the little scuttling crabs that were trying to hide under the stones. Of course, as soon as he caught sight of Henry, he hurried into the water and swam out squa-a-awking. Henry had the unpleasant business of explaining that he hadn't found anything yet, but that if Timothy would please shut up, he would go and try again.

However, Timothy kicked up such a fuss at being left again, that Henry gave up the idea. They settled down to wait, and amused themselves as best they could for whatever he could find, and Henry nibbled at the spider crabs clinging to the kelp stalks. Nasty, disagreeable things they were too, that shouted and clung and nipped to the last swallow.

"Can't we go now?" asked Timothy presently.

And Henry, looking up and seeing the evening star, cool and pale, just over the top of the nearest mountain, decided that they could, especially as he could no longer see the crabs on the kelp stalks.

"Now, don't make a noise!" he cautioned, remembering the commotion he had caused with his last appearance in the bay. And Timothy nodded and blinked his bright little eyes and leaned slightly against the big fin. Now and then he whispered directions, and Henry obeyed, turning left or right as directed.

After a while, however, Henry felt that something was not right. The water was getting shallow, and there was still no sign of Timothy's way out. He was just about to say as much – and more – when there were excited squeaks from his passenger.

"I can see it! I can see it! Straight ahead to your right!"

Henry turned at right angles and went cautiously forward trying to see in the darkness. But as far as he could see, trees loomed in an unbroken circle against the quiet sky. And what was worse, the water was getting still shallower. Henry got more and more uneasy. After all, Timothy was only a seagull. . . .

Then he felt the weeds tickling his tummy, and he knew his vague fears had been right.

"What are you stopping for?" shrieked Timothy, stamping his cold pink toes.

"Because there isn't enough water," said Henry darkly.

"That doesn't matter!" stamped Timothy. "It's only fifty yards across here and then we are right out in the straits."

Henry caught his breath. "Fifty yards of what?" he asked with dark politeness.

"Sand!" shrieked Timothy. "Nice, soft sand! What more do you want?"

So that's what soft pink toes led to: nice soft sand! Henry took a deep breath. There was a south wind blowing and from the sheltered bay they were in he could hear the wind out in the straits piling the waves up against an unseen shore, and as Timothy had said, there was only fifty yards of nice soft sand in between.

He was very quiet. "Get off my back," he said.

And Timothy got.

"Now go on to your straits," he said bitterly.

Timothy started off obediently. But looking back over his shoulder in a bewildered kind of way, he asked, "Aren't you coming too?"

"I can *not* swim in sand!" roared Henry. "Do you think I am a seal?"

"Oh!" said Timothy, wildly trying to shield himself with his one good wing from Henry's furious splashes. "I didn't think of that!"

"You wouldn't!" said Henry, and he added for good measure: "Get out of here!"

And Timothy got—just as fast as he could. Off across the nice soft sand he pattered, very wet and miserable, his broken wing trailing along the ground.

Pad, pad, pad, went the little pink toes—and very pathetic he looked, fading away in the darkness. . . .

Chapter Nine

When Timothy had faded into the dusk, Henry began to back out. It took some time, as it was very weedy, and because he wasn't at all sure of the way he had come. To add to all his troubles, he didn't know whether the tide was high or low, and he knew he might be in very real danger of being stranded. And all because....

No! He'd never think of that seagull again as long as he lived, or of any of the ridiculous things he had made him do. He shut his eyes tight to keep out the unpleasant thoughts, but immediately a procession of little pink toes and fluffy grey feathers padded across his mind.

Then Henry saw something that frightened all thought of grey feathers and pink toes from his mind in one chill rush. As he rounded the point leaving Porpoise Bay, there, directly in front of him, was a tired-looking old fishboat chugging along. The sight of it brought all his mother's warnings back to him at once, and made him realize for the first time the real danger he faced in this dead-end inlet – the danger of being trapped by fishermen, just as Skookum Cecil had been! Then he would never escape this miserable inlet, never see his mother and his friends, never be FREE....

Two men sat in the boat's stern while a third sprawled on top of the deck house lazily steering with his foot. The sight of Henry off the bow brought them to life.

"Hey you guys, look at this! A killer whale!" said the one steering. The men in the stern stood up to look.

"A real monster, he is. I wonder how he got in here?" said one.

"No wonder there's no herring," said the other.

"Herring schmerring," said the steersman. "If we can get the net around that sucker we can take the rest of the year off."

"You already took most of it off without no whale."

"Hey, be serious. Across the line I bet that big fella'd fetch a hunnerd grand," said the steersman, now genuinely excited by his own talk. "I heard on the radio just last month they're looking for a hunnerd killer whales to do some experiment."

"So who's got the permit? You'd look funny tryna smuggle 'im on the bus wrapped in newspaper."

"Trap 'im first, then worry about permits. Say he was tryin' to run up on the sand and we had to save 'im. Use your imagination."

Henry did not understand the men's words but he couldn't have been more terrified if he had. Without another moment's pause he dove and swam as fast and deep as he could. He'd never swum so hard or held his breath so long in his life, but he wanted to put that boat as far behind him as he possibly could. When he finally burst to the surface again the boat was almost out of sight, but Henry was taking no chances. He spouted, bolted another huge breath and again sounded. The next time he surfaced the boat had disappeared completely around the point.

But now a strange feeling had come over Henry and, thrusting forward in the fullness of his enormous strength, he realized how wretchedly cooped-up he'd felt these past days, bumping along the cliff, stopping every few miles to untangle his thoughts. Now the shore was straight and Henry tore along it, frothing up the miles, thinking of the wonderful, bold things that he used to do before he was dragged into this miserable inlet. Fast and furious came the wild free thoughts as he rolled steadily and surely along. In fact, they came so fast that it was hard to think of fishboats or grey feathers and pink toes, or anything else but freedom.

Once he bumped into a seal and muttered an apology before he remembered that he should have eaten it. The seal said nothing, because he really had no words ready for such an occasion. When you bump into a killer whale, words are usually quite unnecessary.

The water was much deeper now, and although Henry didn't know where he was going exactly, he knew he was going to keep straight on. He was wild and free once more, and nothing could stop him.

Dark outlines of cliffs drifted past, but Henry paid no attention to them. He was through with cliffs that led to nowhere, and Roars that never stopped, and seagulls that . . . never mind what. He'd depend on nothing and nobody but himself from now on. He'd get out of it if he had to smash everything in sight. He knew that he had said all this before, but this time, nothing could turn him aside. He'd dive when he liked, and he'd blow when he liked, and he'd make as much noise as he liked – this was a rather narrow passage he was in – and he'd never listen again in his life and go through the Skookum Chuck if he liked, and nothing could stop him . . . unless he liked . . . .

Henry stopped. This was a *very* narrow place! He looked around and raised himself a little farther out of the water to eye it with his bold new look.

Each little ripple seemed to be trying to push the next little ripple . . . lip-lip-lippity-lap-plup . . . and then it would leap over and start pushing the next one. Along the shore, the water was making soft gurgling noises, climbing up the stones as far as it could reach, and then suck-suck-sucking as it drew back again, pulling all the water out of the crevices as it went. Then it would try again a little further along: suck-suck-suck . . . and then hurry off.

Against Henry's sides, it warbled and sang and pushed and pulled. Never had he seen or heard water so eager to get inside him if it could. It played about his mouth; it thrummed through his flippers, and quavered about his tail. Hurry, hurry, hurry lapped the impatient ripples. Gurgle, gurgle, gurgle sang the little swirling eddies. Lippity-lap-lip-lap-lap-lap-lippity-lap hummed the water past his sides. Hurry, hurry, hurry, louder and louder, faster and faster. Suck-suck-burble-burble . . . .

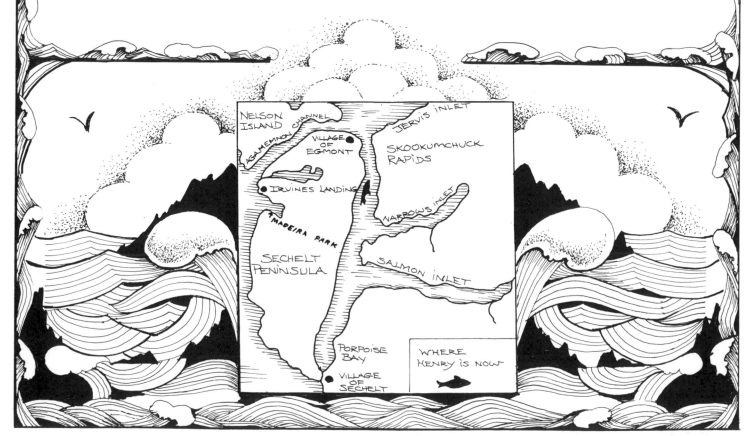

And Henry just lay there wondering and thinking how persistent they were as they tore and fretted against his sides. Then everything kept getting louder and louder, and stronger and more insistent. Still Henry lay there rather enjoying it all.

"It's certainly making enough noise about it," he chuckled. "Roaring like anything!"

Not until he said the word did he realize what was happening. Roaring! Of course it was roaring! And there was only one thing he knew of that could Roar like that, and when it did, he wasn't supposed to be there!

With a terrified bellow, he struck out for safety in the only direction he could, the way the water was going. He knocked the ripples over and sent them flying in all directions. He played havoc with the whirlpools who were only beginning to feel their strength, and the force of his going made the water suck still more greedily at the shores. All the time, the Roar grew steadily louder.

Soon it began to be doubtful whether Henry was knocking the ripples over or the ripples were knocking Henry. And although the whirlpools weren't strong enough yet to suck him down, they were certainly holding their own. And as for the shore — well, the water had no time to suck now as it raced past.

Then slowly the passage broadened out, and the waters took advantage of the extra space to stretch and catch their breath. Henry took advantage of the lull to catch his too, for he knew that the Roar was now quite distinctly behind him. But would it catch up again? Taking no chances, he raced on again.

Cold, misty dawn was breaking now, and it spread over the racing, rumbling, roaring water that followed on Henry's tail. Then into sight came the straggling village, the same village of his mother's lesson, the village where you waited until the Roar stopped. The village where Henry hadn't waited, and so had got into all those troubles. At the sight of it, Henry knew that he was not only safe, but that he was safe at the right end of the Roar. This time, the Skookum Chuck had not dragged him in, it had chased him out.

"Out!" he shouted. "Why, I'm out!" but there was not a sound from the sleeping village to show whether anyone heard or cared.

"Out! Out! Out!" he shouted again to nothing in particular. But the damp grey morning could not rouse a single echo to pass on the news.

Past the rock and small islands. Past the last fishing settlement with its fish-floats . . . .

"Isn't it great? I'm out!" But nothing stirred.

"Pu-ph-e-e-e-ew!" he blew joyfully, as he raced toward the small islet that marks the entrance to Jervis Inlet.

Up rose the tall spar-fin, then sank, then one pointed flange of the great tail . . . and sank. And Henry was gone. Gone back to his own wild free life, and all that remained to mark his going was a great tumult on the surface of the sea.

© 1983 Estate of M. Wylie Blanchet and Harbour Publishing Co. Ltd.
Illustrations © Harbour Publishing Co. Ltd.

3rd Printing, 1989

Printed and bound in Canada.

*Harbour Publishing gratefully acknowledges the contribution of the Canada Council
and the B.C. Cultural Fund.*

Editor: Betty Keller

Canadian Cataloguing in Publication Data

Blanchet, M. Wylie (Muriel Wylie), 1891–1961.
  A whale named Henry.

  Includes index.
  ISBN 0-920080-33-2

  1. Whales – British Columbia – Juvenile fiction.
  I. Title.

PS8553.L35W51983   JC813'.54   C83-091340-8
PZ10.3.B596 Wh 1983

Harbour Publishing Co. Ltd.
P.O. Box 219
Madeira Park, B.C.
VON 2HO